T0193862

PRELUDE
TO THE
CHASE

PRELUDE TO THE CHASE

WM MATTHEW GRAPHMAN

PRELUDE TO THE CHASE

Website: www.matthewgraphman.com
Facebook: facebook.com/SilverwoodChronicles
Instagram: Instagram.com/SilverwoodChronicles

iUniverse books may be ordered through booksellers or by contacting:

iUniverse
1663 Liberty Drive
Bloomington, IN 47403
www.iuniverse.com
1-800-Authors (1-800-288-4677)

ISBN: 978-1-5320-6973-4 (sc)
ISBN: 978-1-5320-6974-1 (e)

Print information available on the last page.

iUniverse rev. date: 02/28/2019

THE SILVERWOOD CHRONICLES

Guardian of TheSilverwood
Book 1

A Spy in Nightfall
Book 2

Prophet to TheOuterlands
Book 3

Friends from Mountain Forge
Book 4

Coming Soon

An Heir Out of Dayspring
Book 5 (Coming Spring 2019)

CHAPTER 1

TAYA

Taya started out each day with the hope that something different or out of the ordinary would happen. Today started out no differently, and as her routine progressed, she knew that she was going to be disappointed yet again. For as long as she could remember, her routine consisted of study, training, eating and sleeping although not necessarily in that order or priority.

While eating and sleeping were as normal as would be expected in their modest abode outside the village of Hydesvalley, her studies and skills training could vary drastically, based on her mentor's mood and expectations. The feeling that today was not going to hold anything new or exciting ran through her head as she faced her opponent.

A hint of sunlight reflected off of her mentor's armor nearly blinding her as she bent backward avoiding the swing of his quarterstaff. Her keen sense of smell noticed the fresh oil on the wood as it passed over her nose by less than the width of her hand. Her balance was shaken but she did notfalter.

"I thought you were using linseed oil on the staffs?" Taya bounced away from her attacker's forward movement.

"I ran out," the tall warrior replied in a matter-of-fact way. She watched as he spun the staff around his shoulder and planted one end of it solidly on the ground. "I grabbed some Berrymore sap. It dries out faster than linseed, but it should work for now."

Taya twisted her own staff in a ready position and released an audible huff. "You almost caught me there, the scent is so strong and not what I was expecting. I nearly lost my balance."

The warrior, whose age was starting to show only in his graying hair, lifted an eyebrow. "In combat, you should always be prepared for the unexpected. Even in war, battles rarely go exactly to plan. It is worthwhile to be aware of subtle differences, but do not allow distractions to cause you to lose focus. The moment you do, you provide the enemy the opening they need."

"I'm only fourteen, I don't know everything, yet," Taya flashed a smile and narrowed her eyes. With a wave of her hand, she invited the next attack.

Twisting his head slightly, a look of confusion washed over her opponent's face as he scanned her figure for a moment. "Fourteen? Has it really been that long?"

Taya did not know whether to laugh at his forgetfulness or cry. "Of course, my birthday is always on the twenty-first day of the month of Obermore. Have you forgotten again?"

"But today is the twentieth day, correct?" He challenged.

"Well, yes," Taya admitted.

"Then I don't feel so bad working you harder today, ahhhh!" With a roar, the large man grabbed his staff and charged at her. With a quick shift, she blocked the charging warrior's staff. Using his momentum, she fell backward and kicked up into his midsection causing him to flip over her.

With a thud, her warrior-mentor hit the ground and let out a groan. "Guardian, are you okay?" Taya rushed over to his prone body.

The man lifted a hand. Taya swallowed and spoke again, "Guntharr, are you okay?"

Guntharr nodded. "Yes, I believe I will live. However, you must hurry and grow up as I am not sure how much longer my services will be of use to you."

"What do you mean?" Taya asked.

"I mean, you and I are at opposite ends of life. Your story is just beginning, and mine is nearing the end," he replied. Taya responded by pursing her lips and cocking her head sideways. A slight lift to one of her eyes announced she was not buying it. Guntharr responded by narrowing his own eyes in a sign of surrender. "Very well, I'm at the later portion of the middle of my story, is that satisfactory?"

"Satisfactory," Taya parroted. She extended a delicate but strong hand toward his and pulled backward with all of her strength as the warrior went from a lying position to a seated position. Her eye fell on a symbol embossed on the left shoulder of his leather tunic which peeked out from under the metal breastplate. The symbol was a large leaf with a war hammer

3

resting in the center. "When are you going to tell me more about your Order?"

"You mean the Guardians?" Guntharr asked.

Taya nodded. "I want to know why you joined them, and what you did? Tell me about all of the places you've seen in Teradandra and the different creatures you've met."

As if on cue, a loud squawk sounded from overhead. Taya looked up and saw a majestic bird whose feathers glowed a deep amber hue. Its wingspan was larger than the length of a horse and as he circled overhead, his large form temporarily blotted out the sun.

"Well you are already familiar with the hawk lords, thanks to Raskin," Guntharr announced.

Taya began a melodic call the sound of which resembled music. Its light and soothing sound carried through the wind as an ember floats carelessly from a raging fire. The bird descended until he touched down on the ground, the beating of his wings slowly softening the landing.

"Is mistress well?" Raskin called in a staccato voice.

Instead of answering, Taya dropped to her knees and wrapped her arms around the feathered creature which stood nearly three foot tall beside her.

"Squawk!" Raskin responded. "Go easy on Raskin. Raskin not rugged like elf and guardian."

Taya laughed at his complaint. "You are virtually indestructible, Raskin, and you know it."

"What brings you in so early, my friend? I did not expect to see you until closer to evening." Guntharr wondered.

"Raskin's day to hunt. Curious what mistress and Guardian want for food," Raskin clarified.

"I will leave that to Taya," Guntharr replied.

Taya had to consider for a moment. Their diet had consisted largely of local vegetables and chicken which Guntharr would procure from the village. Raskin was skilled at hunting lots of different things, but his favorite was field rabbits. Typically, when Raskin took his turn, he would nab two or three rabbits since they were the most convenient. Raskin appreciated the fact that there were several large prairies just on the other side of the river which made his hunt more of a formality than a real chore. He must be in a particularly good mood, Taya considered, as he seldom offered an option.

"Why so accommodating, Raskin?" Taya asked curiously.

"Mistress' hatch-day is tomorrow, is it not? Raskin wants to provide good meal going into special day," Raskin replied.

Taya spun toward the guardian and put her hands gently on his shoulders. "You see, even Raskin remembered my hatch-day."

"You were not hatched, you were born," Guntharr corrected her.

Taya shoved with all of her strength sending the guardian backward with a thud. She stood and paced around her hawk lord companion and considered for a moment. She always enjoyed doing this as she would often watch from the corner of her eye to see just how far the hawk lord could turn his head before having to swivel it back around the other way.

Running her fingers through her long white hair as she thought for a moment. "Since you are asking, it's been a long time since we've had deer."

Raskin released an elongated squawk which sounded more like a scream. "Mistress is joking?"

Guntharr held up a finger, "In all fairness, you did not provide any boundaries on your offer."

Raskin blinked not once but twice, which was something he seldom did. Taya folded her arms and frowned. "Maybe Raskin find a small doe for Mistress."

"What? Don't you think you can find a deer? They are large four-footed creatures with sleek, long brown bodies. The males will often have . . ." Taya teased.

"Raskin know deer." Raskin twisted his head so that one eye focused directly on her. "Raskin can find, but Raskin never tried to carry something that big. Maybe Raskin hunt and kill, and Guardian fetch?"

Taya chuckled softly, "I don't think that's how it works," she pressed.

Raskin hopped closer to Guntharr. "Guardian would not mind, would Guardian?" Raskin shook slightly, several feathers falling to the ground.

Guntharr dipped his head slightly which Taya understood to be a hearty nod. "I suppose a compromise can be arranged given that this could work as Taya's birthday meal."

Raskin extended his wings, flapping them several times and then clicked his beak together. "Raskin help make hatching day, the best one yet!"

"I didn't really hatch, but you have the right idea," Taya began to correct him.

"I find a sweet doe for celebration and bring it back . . . maybe," Raskin said with determination.

"If you find it's more than you can handle," Guntharr interrupted, "you know where to find us. I can always grab a skiff and drag it back."

With a flurry of dust, the Hawk Lord ascended with grace into the blue sky and sailed off in search of the perfect kill.

"As I was saying," Taya returned to her previous thought.

"What was that?" Guntharr acted forgetfully. Taya knew better. While she had not encountered many individuals outside of Hydesvalley, none compared with her Guardian. Forgetfulness was not in his makeup. She had heard him recall details of various encounters that she did not know that she had even forgotten.

"You know exactly what we were talking about. I want to know more about some of the other races you have encountered on your journeys through the five realms," she prompted.

"Grab your bow and I will cover some highlights while you are practicing," Guntharr conceded.

7

Taya was never very comfortable with fighting with her staff, but Guntharr felt she needed to get better with it before she could take up the sword. On more than one occasion, Guntharr had shown her various stances and attacks, but her focus had been mostly on using her bow or staff. Of the two, she felt most comfortable with her bow. During her many hours of practice each day, her time with her bow was not only the most productive but also felt the most natural.

Taya took off in a sprint toward the back of the cottage which she and Guntharr had called home for most of her life. The structure was simple but special. She never understood the significance of it, and Guntharr seemed a little elusive whenever the question of its history came up. He would always say that it was a good strong house that had weathered the sands of time better than he had. It certainly had character. The stonework was amazing. Unlike the common peasant home, this structure's stones had been hand-carved and put into place. They were not uniform, but they shared common craftsmanship that distinguished it from any other structure she had seen. It was as if the house had been constructed for royalty, but not a gaudy, flashy royalty. This was a type of royalty that was devoted to function over form. Whoever had originally laid the stone for this cottage clearly had the resources to build something much larger, but decided not to.

Before entering in through the door, she expertly tossed the staff into the rack which stood off to the one side. Not waiting for the confirmation that it had reached its proper storage location, she pushed through the door with her mind set on the main dining area. She knew she would find what she was looking for there.

As expected, her bow was still resting against the large wooden table from the night before. Her hands were still soft from the wax she had used on the bowstring from the night before. Snatching it up, she dashed around the end of the table and then across the room. Against the far wall, a chest sat on the floor with its lid closed. Taya flung the lid open, reached in, and pulled out the quiver, spilling some of the arrows it held inside the large wooden box. Her motions were so rushed that the lid to the locker slipped closed before she could catch it. A loud snapping sound echoed throughout the room as the lid crashed down on several of the protruding arrow shafts.

Taya released a frustrated and audible sigh. She knew the guardian would be upset if he saw her bouncing around like a leaf caught in a crosswind. He would particularly be disappointed if she managed to shatter one of the arrows. Carefully lifting the lid, she rescued the arrows that had been trapped by the falling lid. A systematic examination of each arrow confirmed that the sound she had heard was the arrows slapping the inside of the locker and nothing else.

Stuffing her quiver until it could hold no more, she slung it over her shoulder and dashed out the door. Upon stepping outside, she saw that the Guardian was no longer standing where they had been sparring which meant he had already moved over the hill to the range. Taking full advantage of the moment, she stretched out her stride and sprinted as fast as she could across the ridge overlooking the river valley below and up the slope to the crest of the hill where the guardian had set up her shooting range.

Looking across a slight recess in the terrain, she spotted Guntharr adjusting the positions of a couple of the targets. An acknowledging glance from him indicated that he saw her arrival. He appeared to be checking the stability of a specific target, then he turned and began jogging in her direction. It didn't take him long to cover the hundred and twenty feet, passing several additional targets along the way. Each one received a quick inspection as he passed by.

"Was there something wrong?" Taya asked as he approached.

"No. I was just making some minor adjustments to increase the difficulty," Guntharr admitted.

"Why?" Taya was skilled at hitting the furthest target, but she was not an expert yet, at least not in her eyes.

"Some growth happens organically," Guntharr answered. "Time is all that is required and simple nurturing. Real strength only comes through stretching one's ability beyond what is considered normal. Do you notice anything different about the farthest target?"

Taya looked across the range at the target Guntharr had been focused on when she arrived. Now that he mentioned it, it was different. It was now smaller, somehow. A moment passed and it occurred to her what he had been doing. The Guardian had rotated the target face perpendicular to the range thereby making the face of the target now smaller by one quarter.

"I see what you did. You turned it slightly. It shouldn't be that much harder to hit," Taya argued.

"By all means, proceed," Guntharr waved a hand in the direction of the target.

Taya snatched an arrow from her quiver and knocked it securely to the freshly waxed bowstring. She pulled back with a steady, fluid motion and focused her attention on the familiar target downrange. As per her training, she closed out the many distractions around her. As she focused, she could easily make out the markings on the target which represented the center even from this angle. With the arrow at the ready, she began to realize the full difference the Guardian's adjustment had made.

A surge of determination rushed through her as she forced an adjustment to her aim as a gentle breeze crossed over her fingertips. Taking a breath, she allowed the string to slip from her grasp sending the arrow streaking toward its intended target. With her expert eyes, she followed the arrow to its destination. Disappointment struck home as she watched the arrow strike the center of the target and ricochet off, hurtling down the hill.

"But I was dead on!" Taya protested as a few blades of straw drifted from the target to the ground.

"You would have been, had you stood twenty feet in that direction," the Guardian corrected her. "As it is, the angle of the target works in the target's defense. Not only is it smaller, but the energy in your arrow is also easily redirected."

"You knew that would happen," Taya concluded.

Guntharr tipped his head slightly.

"Is there a way to compensate for it?" Taya asked.

"Indeed. Hand me an arrow," Guntharr stretched out his hand and awaited her response.

Taya reached back into her quiver and pulled out a fresh arrow.

"I have taught you that an arrow does not naturally fly in a perfectly flat or straight pattern."

11

"Yes, you taught me long ago that a launched arrow has a tendency to wiggle as it travels through the air," Taya responded and handed over the arrow.

"Correct. The solution is to force the arrow to wiggle, as you say, in your favor such that when it strikes the center of the target it is actually arching in the direction necessary." Guntharr examined the fletching on the end of the shaft. Wetting his fingers, he ruffled one of the veins. With careful precision, he caused the vein to bend slightly. "Now, try this. Remember to aim the same way as you did previously, but drawback as if you are shooting just beyond the target."

Taya accepted the modified arrow. She studied the alterations and committed the slight bend to memory. Nodding her understanding, she checked her stance, knocked the arrow, and drew back on the bowstring. Following her training, she eyed her target and took note of any variation in the wind. Recalling Guntharr's instruction, she pulled back farther, overdrawing the bowstring slightly. This raised a slight concern. Because of the added power, there was a greater risk of overshooting her target.

But she learned long ago, that the Guardian's experience and knowledge were nearly without flaw. One more check on the wind and she released the arrow. As before, she followed the path of the arrow but panicked as the arrow began a wide bank to her right. Time slowed to a crawl as Taya watched the arrow fly widely off course. Just as she was about to shout an objection, the arrow curved sharply at the last moment. The arrow flew straight into the center of the target at precisely the right angle.

"Satisfactory," Guntharr commented.

"That . . . that was amazing," Taya responded. "You have got to teach me how to do that!"

"In time," he replied. "For today, focus on the midrange targets," he instructed.

"The wind up here is a bit tricky," Taya added. "I'm still not sure why we moved farther away from the house."

Taya knew she had missed something the moment Guntharr lifted an eyebrow. "We moved precisely because of the wind. You must learn to always take the elemental conditions into account with every shot. Nearer our home, the wind is less noticeable and you had all but mastered every target."

"Yes, Guardian," Taya smiled.

"And now, let's entertain your earlier question," Guntharr continued.

Taya took a deep breath and pulled out another arrow. She fixed her stance and aimed at the second farthest target. "What question was that? I forgot what we were talking about before the whole arrow thing."

"You had asked me about some of the various races I had encountered in Teradandra," Guntharr replied. "Let me tell you about some of my favorite beings in all of the five realms, the Battle Wolves."

CHAPTER 2

RIFT

Rift was nearing the village of Brittle after being on the road for many weeks. The journey had been much longer than he had remembered. Maybe, it was because he was taking it easy, or it could be that he was getting older and slower. In either case, he would be very happy to see his old friend, Firebane. His sabbatical away from the council of wolves was long overdue. Only after his son, Lightning Fang, was permitted to assume his seat at the council, was he given permission to leave the valley.

Shimmer, his mate of thirty years, was reluctant to let him go at first, but he reassured her that he could take care of himself. After all, he was Thunderpack's Clan Lord. Very few in Wolf Valley or even in Mountain Forge would dare challenge him. At least, that was the image he tried to portray. Rift knew that reality was a little different. Twenty, ten or even seven years ago, there was very little he feared, but now, just two seasons before he broke forty years of age, Rift was more unsure of his abilities than ever before.

The journey from his den to Brittle had been nearly four weeks long, and the One True God had provided him a safe and uneventful trip up to this point. Once at the church in Brittle, Father Firebane would provide him with sanctuary and refreshment along with an opportunity to meditate and study. It was a common misconception that Battle Wolves' sole pastime was fighting. While it was true that some wolves lived to fight, his life journey had shown him that knowledge was much more fulfilling than blood.

His plan was to stay for two months and then head back to Wolf Valley and turn over his seat to whomever the council would elect. Deep in his heart, he felt like Lightning Fang was ready, but ultimately the council would decide. They could theoretically pick someone from another family, but that would be the first time that someone from Rift's line had not held the title of Clan Lord in over two centuries. Regardless, he would then live out the remaining few years of his life basking in the sun and watching the young wolf pups play in the river.

"What do we have here, boys?" Rift stopped instantly as three humans stepped out from a large thicket that protruded next to the road. Rift was surprised not so much by their sudden appearance, but that his nose did not alert him to their presence a mile ago. He realized he had been truly lost in thought.

Each of the humans brandished a small sword. Only the one that spoke held it in his hands, the others seemed content just to have a hand on the hilt. They each wore tattered robes with crusted leather tunics underneath.

"Looks like we have ourselves a prize," the second human announced with a smile revealing several missing teeth.

15

"Trust me, fellows, I'm no prize," Rift casually announced. "You would be lucky if you could pay someone to take my scruffy pelt."

"What do you know?" The third human spoke. "The fuzzy little wolf thinks he knows his own worth."

Rift considered his next move. Did these amateurs realize they were talking to a Battle Wolf? He could turn these goons into buzzard chow in just a few minutes if he wanted to, but he reminded himself he was on vacation and he would do everything he could to avoid a fight this close to his destination.

"Maybe I do, maybe I don't," Rift chuckled. "But what I do know, you don't want to mess with this fuzzy little wolf. I've been on the road for weeks and I'm almost at my destination, so let's not ruin a nearly perfect trip."

Before Rift could react, the third human pulled a net from his back and tossed it over the wolf. He really had hoped he could have avoided this, but it looked like things would have to get messy. As it was, the net was bulky enough to keep him from running away, but not such that it would keep him quiet. Rift lifted his head and began to let out a monstrous howl.

"That's his transformation howl, stop him!" The first human shouted in response.

The howl triggered a surge of energy that coursed through his entire being, but it had no sooner begun than one of the humans tackled the wolf knocking the wind from him. The second human grabbed two strands of the net and began pulling it tighter forcing his muzzle closed. This meant only one thing, these ruffians knew what type of wolf he was and they were prepared to keep him from uttering his battle prayer at all cost.

Rift tried to fight back. He tried thrashing his head back and forth but the restraint prevented all but the slightest of movements. He tried kicking with his hind legs and scratching with his front, but the net had already been drawn down tight and any leverage he had was lost. Had he just a few more seconds to complete his prayer, then things would be very different.

"Tie him down, Crastian," the leader directed.

Rift observed which human responded and made a mental note that it was the human sporting almost no fur – not that humans had much fur compared to wolves. The hair Crastian had was as black as oil. He was very muscular as humans go, and his eyes were a brilliant green color. He wore no real armor, only a basic leather shirt which would protect from simple hazards.

"Almost got it. Jorgan, slip the cap over the beast's snout," Crastian directed the third human.

Jorgan was a short fellow, Rift noted. Scraggly brown fur, or what humans callhair, hung down from the crown of his head to just below his shoulders. Rift estimated Jorgan hadn't bathed in some time judging from the human's odor and griminess. Rift saw a small opportunity as Jorgan neared with a tube-shaped hood made of leather and laced up with heavy cords.

"You're going to have to relax it just a bit so I can get it through the netting," Jorgan dropped down near Rift's head.

At the moment that Crastian loosened his grip, Rift kicked with his hind legs and jerked his head to one side. There was just enough slack that Rift's motion knocked Jorgan off balance. Snapping wildly at the human, Jorgan, caught off guard by the sudden viciousness, backed up a step.

"What are you doing?" The first human asked. "If my name isn't Braidest, you are the two most incompetent poachers. . ."

"Quit your preaching and get a hold of him!" Crastian shouted.

Rift knew this was the moment if there was to be one, "Ah-Hooooooooooo!"

Crastian tried desperately to pull the net tight but the wolf's previous actions resulted in the net being twisted. The wolf's battle prayer caused him to double and then triple in size which stretched the net further such that it was ripped from the poacher's hands. Rift stood upright, his form now the size of a horse.

"Swords!" Braidest ordered.

"I wouldn't do that if I were you," Rift suggested, his once gravelly voice now deep like an ocean's roar.

Jorgan chuckled, "you seem to forget, you are still wearing a net."

Rift considered this as Crastian neared his flank almost close enough for a swing. Rift opened his massive mouth, bearing his dagger-like teeth. "Grrrr!"

Crastian instinctively backed away for a moment. Rift knew that if he was to get on even footing, he was going to have to get out of this net.

Jorgan and Braidest drew their swords and advanced on the encumbered battle wolf. He had only seconds to make a decision. Thrashing his head and body back and forth the net that once hung to the ground inched its way up around the wolf's back. This might be enough slack to do what he needed to do.

"Look, the lone battle wolf is shaking with fear," Braidest mocked.

Rift felt the fire inside well up such that had he been a different kind of wolf, he might just roast the human where he stood, but instead, he used what ability he had. "I'm not just a lone battle wolf," Rift snarled. "I am Rift, Clan Lord of Thunderpack. And you just ruined an otherwise uneventful trip." Now free enough to take a few steps forward, Rift triggered his gift. Each battle wolf born is given a unique ability that can be activated when they are in battle form. His gift allowed him to instantaneously move in the direction he was already going through objects at an accelerated rate. Flashing out of existence, the net, now held up by nothing but air, fell to the ground.

"Where did he go?" Jorgan remarked looking around.

"Right behind you," Rift's ominous voice barked from behind the poacher.

All three of the humans stared in disbelief. "How in the world?" Crastian's voice squeaked.

"Attack him, idiots," Braidest shouted.

Jorgan reacted by half swinging at Rift. Rift turned his massive head sideways and caught the blade in his teeth. "Unnn-ahhhh." Rift mumbled, his mouth full of sword. Lifting his right paw, he swatted at the human and sent him tumbling across the ground without his sword. Turning his head, Rift spat out the sword.

Crastian, seeing his fallen comrade, charge at Rift, his sword held high above his head. Rift dove forward turning sideways slightly and rolling on his shoulders and back. The human tried to avoid the large rolling object, but Rift's outstretched front leg caught him and knocked him flat. The momentum from Rift's dive had allowed him to pop back up on his feet.

"Now, it's just you and me," Rift growled.

Braidest observed that his two comrades were not getting up anytime soon and decided that it was probably not a good idea to go one-on-one with a battle wolf. Rift watched as the human dropped his sword in surrender and took off running for cover.

For a moment, Rift had considered taking off after the poacher and teaching him a lesson. It would have been easy. He would have caught up with the human in just a few seconds, but he decided that he had wasted enough time and should finish his journey.

With a stride nearly the equal of a galloping horse, Rift took off down the road continuing toward his destination. After several minutes of running, Rift could feel his energy level beginning to wane. It was not good for him to stay in battle form for too long. While incredibly powerful in this form, it was extremely taxing on his real form. Slowing to a walk, Rift began his transformation howl again and step by step, his form returned to that of a normal wolf.

"Well, that was fun," Rift thought sarcastically to himself as fatigue washed over him.

The little village of Brittle loomed just over the rise of the next hill. His destination was not the village itself, but rather the large sanctuary on the far side that was dedicated to the One True God which his longtime friend Father Firebane pastored. He and Firebane had served together many years before with the Guardian Corps alongside a particularly stoic Guardian whose name escaped him at the moment.

Rift continued toward the village, sifting through the memories back to when he had last seen that Guardian. It must have been at least ten years prior. No, it was longer because Spire Tree, the fortress of Silverwood, fell to the Talicrons nearly fourteen years before. That meant it had been at least seventeen years prior. Rift shuttered at the realization that his father been gone so long. It was at the death of his father when he had taken up the mantle of Clan Lord.

And now, here he was less than a dozen years away from joining his father and grandfather in the great paradise beyond Teradandra in the presence of the One True God. In some respects, he was ready. Life had been hard these last fourteen years since Silverwood's fall. Without the King, factions from all corners of the five realms fought to gain control over this or that.

Clan Thunderpack, along with most of the battle wolves, still held to the hope that one day an heir to the throne would return and establish peace across the land, but there were many that saw this as an opportunity to create havoc. Not far from his home in Wolf Valley, his nearest neighbors in Mountain Forge, the Hawk Lords, had all but given in to the chaos. On more than one occasion they had threatened to start a war with the battle wolves over the plains of Eddiforth along with the eastern edge of the Volcanic Mountains which bordered the plains. Until now, they had avoided it through diplomatic means, but the time was running out before the inevitable would happen.

It was the involvement in all of that local politics that drove him to seek this sabbatical. For now, his son would tend to his clan's needs in his stead. Lightning Fang was a capable young wolf. While he did not yet garner the respect of the other clan leaders, they knew that should anything go awry, that Rift would hold them all to account, and so they agreed to let him go on this last journey.

As the sun grew tired on the horizon, Rift approached the large wooden doors to the main citadel. He was not surprised that they were closed at this time of the evening as the risk of rogue creatures increased as nightfall drew closer. Rift started out by pawing at the door and waited.

He allowed a minute or more to go by and then he repeated his version of a knock. It was times like this, that he envied humans, elves and other two-legged creatures. The closest he could come to a true knock would involve him throwing his shoulder into the door repeatedly, and he was already beyond exhaustion as a result of his run-in with the poachers.

After a third attempt and no response, Rift decided to do the only other thing he knew he could do to attract the attention of those inside. Throwing his head back, Rift allowed the energy flow through him and into his prayer howl. As he began to grow, the howl likewise grew. First, the sound simply resonated off the wooden doors, but slowly as he neared his climax, the ground and walls of the citadel began to vibrate with the sound of his howl.

Within seconds of completing his transformation, the door snapped open and a tall ruddy human stood wearing a dark robe and carrying a sizable staff with a white crystal in the shape of a flame of fire mounted in the crown of the staff. The face, though lined with age, was familiar to him. The man's hair once black as oil now appeared to have salt sprinkled liberally throughout it.

"As the One True God lives, if it isn't my good friend Rift," the robed figure smiled broadly.

"Firebane, it has been a long time," Rift's mighty voiced boomed.

Firebane looked around with concern. "Is there a problem? Why the battle form?"

In the excitement of the moment of seeing his friend, Rift had forgotten that he was still in his battle form. "Oops. No problem." Rift started his transformation knowing that this second use of his conversion was not going to end well. As he returned to his normal self, Rift could feel all of his remaining strength start to leave him. "Tried knocking, but no answ . . ." Rift felt his legs give out and he started to topple over.

Firebane caught and cradled him in his arms. "Tronic, Phandor! Bring a blanket and some water."

Rift struggled to open his eyes and look at his friend. "Came . . . to . . . rest."

"Yes," Firebane petted him on the top of his head.

"You know I hate being petted," Rift remembered mumbling before darkness started to envelop him.

"Rest, Rift. Rest," Rift heard the priest say as he drifted off to sleep.

CHAPTER 3

SCRAG

S crag hesitated as he reached for the handle to the heavy wooden door that was ornately carved from top to bottom with images of angels and dragons at war with one another. This door always gave him pause, not because of the incredible scene that it portrayed, but rather, the uncertainty that lay beyond it. Every time he crossed its threshold, he knew it could be his last day in this existence.

Like his father before him and his father's father, Scrag had served the mistress to pay off a lifetime of debt incurred by his family as did many others like him. He could not recall the reason for the debt, although he knew that the repayment of it would not happen in his lifetime, and possibly not even his children's lifetime. His mistress made certain to remind all that were in her service of this at every opportunity.

The challenge was to make sure that whatever required interrupting her day was worth the risk of dying for. On more than one occasion, Scrag had witnessed other messengers, like himself, enter into the mistress' presence with unfavorable or ill-timed news. In almost every one of these occasions, Scrag was forced to sweep up the ashes of what remained of the messenger. All in all, his mistress was generous, but she had a fiery temper both figuratively and literally, and it was never a good thing to be on the receiving end of that temper.

This is why he stood unmoving as he had so many times before. Once he was admitted into the library beyond the ornate door, which is where his mistress spent most of her day, Scrag had better be sure he had a good reason for being there.

He forced another glace at the note which he had received while in his sleeping hut just outside of the main estate grounds. The note itself was not special in and of itself; at least Scrag did not think so. But then again, Scrag did not read the human tongue nor did he read the writings of his own people, the goblins. The truth was Scrag could not read at all, which for a creature in his position was not all that surprising. Scrag had been trained as a scout and assassin. His specialty was more in keeping an eye on things or killing things. There were other goblin castes that handled more of the brainy stuff, like the shamans. Goblins were identified very early on as either having the gift of magic or not. Those goblins that did not respond to magic ended up being trained in battle while the others earned the privilege of learning.

No, what made the note so special was how it had appeared to him. A large camp of mud huts had been erected by his people centuries before outside the estate grounds. Here is where he grew up, as did most of his associates. There were enough goblins in the camp that nothing or no one should have been able to enter any one of their huts unseen or unheard. But someone had managed to do so this very night in his own hut.

Scrag had not seen whoever it was, but he had heard the voice. It was a low, commanding voice that seemed to echo from every shadow in his humble hut. It informed him of a note that rested on the small table, carved from a log, beside his cot. Scrag lit a candle and tried to scan the room, but any time the light touched the shadow, the candle would extinguish itself even though there was no wind. This puzzled Scrag. Though the huts were unsightly by human standards, they were still quite solid. The absence of a breeze was common, and last night the air was still and quiet.

"You serve the mistress, Naranda," the voice stated matter-of-factly.

"Who's there?" Scrag asked.

"One who shares a common interest with your mistress."

"Why Scrag not see you?" Scrag picked up the single lit candle and began to direct it toward the corner of the room where the voice seemed to originate from. But rather than reveal the source of the voice, the candle, as well as the light that radiated from it, seemed to get pulled into the darkness until the candle was extinguished.

"Little goblin, do not try to find me," the voice ordered, "you do not need to see me, only listen."

Scrag noticed that the voice had shifted position from where it had first spoken. Now he was tremendously confused. Even in the dark, goblins could usually see the energy radiating from a living being, but Scrag saw nothing. "Scrag think the voice in my head the result of bad meat from dinner, not real."

"Extend the candle over your table, Scrag."

Scrag considered the request and decided to do as suggested and his hand hovered over the small table, the candle bursting into flame revealing a folded parchment.

"Did your imagination just make the candle ignite or parchment appear?"

Scrag considered this for a moment and decided that his imagination was good, but not that good. "How you do this? Scrag met elves not this good at mastering shadow."

"Oh, I assure you, there are elves capable of this and much more, but you would never know it," the voice shifted once again.

"So, you are an elf?"

"Ha haha, no. I am no elf, but I have studied under some of the greatest and I have even mastered that which the elves dare not."

"What does non-elf want with Scrag?" Scrag was losing interest in his conversation with nothingness.

"Pick up the letter."

Scrag began to reach down to pick up the parchment and stopped short. Something did not seem right. Scrag suspected a trap or maybe a joke being played out by one of his mistress' many strange guests.

"What is the matter, goblin?"

"Scrag suspect he being pranked," he pulled his hand back and the candle subsequently went out.

"Tsk, tsk, tsk. Naranda has really subdued you. How unfortunate."

Scrag detected an honest sympathy in the voice. He also picked up on some subtle but clearly defined footsteps behind him. He spun quickly and reached out into the darkness, but found nothing.

"Dark Goblins were once considered the most resourceful and insightful assassins in the East."

"Scrag resourceful. Scrag very insightful," Scrag responded.

"Oh, I don't doubt that you were, but your reluctance to brave a plain piece of paper would indicate that maybe you are not as regal as I had been told. No matter, I will search out another goblin more suited to a truly heroic task."

Scrag felt anger welling up inside him. "Scrag heroic. Scrag most heroic in mistress' service. You need something heroic done, Scrag your goblin."

"Then deliver my message to your mistress," was the simple reply.

"Now Scrag know he being pranked. Delivering message to mistress not heroic, it more like rolling dice against death," Scrag scoffed.

The voice seemed to vanish for a moment before returning. "The delivery itself is not a heroic act, it's the message within that could determine the fate of your mistress and all of Teradandra."

"Why non-elf not give it, himself? If non-elf can hide from Scrag, he could certainly do the same with mistress," Scrag admitted.

There was a pause in the conversation and Scrag was sure he heard the voice sigh. "Let's just say that I am not open to confronting Naranda at this time for much the same reason as you hesitate every time you approach her door."

This statement Scrag could appreciate, but that only meant that he would be the target of any displeasure and not the voice in hiding. "Scrag not feeling like helping non-elf out."

Behind him, Scrag heard an odd clanking sound as if someone had dropped a bunch of metal together.

"Consider this a token of my appreciation, goblin," the voice faded away.

Scrag spun around and saw a small pouch nestled in the corner of the hut. Running over, he opened the sack to discover a large collection of gold coins, more than he had ever seen, at least this close. There must have been more than a dozen coins in there. Scrag could not count much higher than that.

"Forty, my bewildered dark friend. There are forty gold coins in the pouch, just for you. All for simply delivering my message to your mistress."

Scrag did not really care where the voice was at this point, all he cared about was this incredible treasure which had just been handed to him. "Nothing more, just deliver the message?"

"That's it and all that coin is yours."

"Scrag don't have to share with anyone?" Scrag wanted to confirm.

"Ha haha! Bury it, give it away, or spend it on good food and drink, I don't care. It is yours and nobody else's."

"What if mistress finds out?" Scrag wondered.

"I'm certainly not going to tell her. This is between you and me," the voice began to fade. "Now, don't disappoint me or I'll have to return and next time I won't be playing games and bearing gifts."

Scrag did not want to waste any more time. He stretched his hand over the table searching for the note, and as he did, the candle erupted into life once more. The sudden appearance startled the goblin such that he jerked back almost knocking the candle onto the floor. The additional light revealed that the message was no longer on the stand where he last saw it. Scrag panicked, what had happened to the message? If he did not deliver the message right away, the voice would return and take the gold away from him.

His eyes darted all around the hut looking for any sign of the parchment. As despair began to overtake him, the faded yellow corner of parchment caught his eye as it poked out from under the edge of his cot.

"Let's get you to mistress before Scrag loses you again," Scrag scolded the paper.

Scrag stepped through the door of the hut and stopped. He turned around and rushed back in, snatching the bag of coins. "Must not let others find Scrag's treasure."

After considering his options, he walked over to his cot and stuffed the bag between the layers of furs and straw that made up his humble bed.

Satisfied that his gold was safe for the moment, he scampered out the door and across the muddy field that bordered the large estate, resting on top of the ridge. It was late in the evening, so the fact that light radiated from the massive structure in front of him was no surprise. The reality was there were only a handful of people that actually lived in the structure which made Scrag wonder why so much light was needed. But that was not of his concern, or so his mistress would say.

There were a few of his comrades roaming outside of their huts as he trekked across the make-shift village and up the side of the hill. As he neared the top, there was a tall stone fence that circled the house with only two entrances. The front was the larger entrance made up of iron gates. They were heavily guarded by goblins and possessed a magical lock that could only be opened by a stone kept in the gatekeeper's pouch.

The rear entrance, reserved for Scrag and the hired help, was much humbler. The opening in the stonework was about the size of a human. The only path to this opening was through the field of goblin huts where Scrag and the others that served the mistress, lived. The gate, like its larger more ornate counterpart, was similarly guarded and locked. The ground just beyond the gate, should someone try to sneak through, was littered with traps. Scrag knew where they all were, but he took his time to navigate it so as not to leave a clear trail for an intruder.

As he approached the small gate, the guards on duty immediately recognized him and stood to attention.

"What Scrag doing up so late?" A gnarly old goblin asked. He held a curved sword that looked slightly larger than he could handle, but he managed to twirl it around with competence and ease.

"Let Scrag pass, Krog. Scrag needs to see mistress."

The two goblins laughed with a chuckle that was a blend of metal scratching against stone and hiccups. Their response also reinforced the dire threat to his life that Scrag was about to undertake for a sack of gold.

Scrag began to rethink this endeavor. Was he sure he wanted to go through with this? After all, it was just a bag of gold coins. An image of the bag popped into his mind. His courage began to swell as the thought of what all that money could do for him.

"Stand aside," Scrag ordered.

The laughing goblins quickly sobered up at the order from their commanding officer. Their faces reflected the fact that whatever it was that Scrag needed to see the mistress about, it must be serious enough to risk his life.

Stepping to the side, the goblin Krog pulled a small, dull looking gem from a pouch attached to his belt and placed it inside a small indentation on the gate. After a brief flash of light radiated from the stone, the gate swung open. Scrag nodded in appreciation and hurried on past the gate. Navigating the trapped courtyard with ease, Scrag made it to the back entrance of the house without further incident.

Scrag hammered at the door knowing that it was locked from the inside and waited patiently for the porter to answer his summons. Seconds turned into minutes and Scrag began to pace about. Frustrated, Scrag pounded on the door once again, this time with slightly more ferocity than before.

The door eventually opened revealing a tall, thin human male who was in the upper years of his life.

"There are other duties I attend to besides letting you in and out," the well-dressed fellow charged in a level tone.

"Scrag must see mistress. Got important message for her. Henry let Scrag in?"

Scrag registered the gentleman's concern as he took in a deep breath and exhaled audibly.

"Lady Naranda is currently in her study. She wanted to spend some time alone reading before retiring for the evening and did not wish to be disturbed," Henry reported.

Scrag considered this for a moment and almost opted to turn around, but he nodded in understanding. This would be something he would be willing to risk his neck for.

"Very well," Henry stepped aside and allowed Scrag to enter. "If I do not hear you leave in the next fifteen minutes, I'll be sure to bring up a broom to the library to sweep up your remains."

"Scrag hope that not necessary."

He did not look back as he made his way through the pristine halls and up the wide curving staircase to the second floor. At the top of the stairs stood the large ornate door to the mistress' study. Scrag closed his eyes and took a deep breath. Resisting the urge to barge in, knowing that would most certainly get him fried, he carefully tapped on the door and awaited the response.

Unlike the back door to the house, Scrag knew well enough that knocking more than once was not only unnecessary but also unwise. The worst Henry would provide was a good verbal beat-down, however, Lady Naranda was capable of magical feats that caused Scrag to shutter.

Seconds became minutes. As the minutes clicked by in Scrag's head, he began to wonder if maybe the mistress had already turned in for the evening. If that was the case, then all was lost. He did not dare disturb her while she was resting.

Scrag considered his options and decided that he might need to tap on the door one more time, even though it would not likely end well. As he raised his bony hand to the door a soft and refined voice sounded from the inside.

"Come," the female voice ordered.

Exhaling, Scrag reached for the handle and pushed the door open slowly.

"Who is there?" Naranda asked in a controlled fashion.

"Scrag, mistress," Scrag pushed himself into the room and closed the door gently behind him.

The room was well lit as were most of the rooms in the large estate. Several towering candle stands were scattered throughout the room that was large enough to sleep thirty goblins, were it converted to a barracks. Instead of goblins, this room was the home to shelves loaded with books from floor to ceiling. In one corner of the room sat a large wooden desk, carved with the same skill and craftsmanship as the ornate door. Surrounding the desk were three wooden high-back chairs, trimmed with delicate, red fabric. Sitting in one of those chairs, almost profile to Scrag, sat an attractive woman – at least from a human's standpoint so he had heard. The Lady Naranda was somewhere in her early forties, but as far as Scrag could tell, bore the youthful appearance of one ten years her junior. She wore a blood red gown that caused her to almost blend into the fabric of the chair where she was seated. Were it not for her ivory skin and dark velvet hair, Scrag would have missed her completely.

She folded the book that rested in her lap and lay it gently on the corner of the desk beside her. Pulling herself upright, she stood probably a foot taller than the goblin. "Well."

Scrag bowed respectfully. "Scrag bring a special message for the mistress."

Her eyebrows lowered and her previously inconvenienced look was slowly replaced with an annoyed look. "What is so special about this message that you would disturb me in my study?"

Scrag immediately realized he had made a critical error. Now, he would have to divulge where the message came from and possibly even tell her about the gold he had been paid to deliver it.

He decided he would try to outwit his mistress instead. "It special, because Scrag found it in his hut tonight." Scrag extended the hand holding the note in Naranda's direction.

From the other side of the room, Naranda dismissed the note with the wave of her hand. "So, a piece of paper appears in your hut, and you assume it is for me because?"

Scrag felt himself shrinking back as he spoke, "because voice in the shadows told him it was for you." It was out before he could stop himself and Scrag knew he was in big trouble.

To his surprise, Scrag's reaction drew a chuckle from the lady of the house and not anger. "Oh Scrag, have you been sampling some of that awful goblin grog that they cook up outside?"

Scrag straightened up at the accusation. "No mistress, Scrag not drink that awful stuff as mistress does not permit such things of her captains." He again extended the note.

Her half-formed smile was replaced by a frown. "Bring it here."

Scrag walked softly across the rug that adorned the wooden floor over to the chair where Naranda sat. As he got within arm's reach, she extended her open hand. Scrag placed the note in her hand as carefully as a mother might lay a sleeping baby in its bed.

Naranda turned the paper over in her hand multiple times as if searching for something. "Is this a joke?"

Panicked, Scrag scurried back. "No, why?"

"There is no message here, you stupid goblin. You have disturbed me for the last time," Naranda rose to her feet; her hands began to glow red.

As the flames began to coalesce around Naranda's hands, Scrag noticed markings begin to appear on the paper she held. These were not burn markings as he suspected at first, but something else.

"Look," Scrag begged, pointing at the paper.

Naranda's eyes followed the goblins long skinny finger to the note. Immediately, her expression changed and the flames faded from her hands. "A message indeed."

Sitting back in her chair, Naranda began uttering the words to a simple spell, and she passed her hand over the blank page, once again. Upon her command, the image of letters began to form. She studied the note for some time before turning her attention back to the goblin.

"Where did you get this?" She demanded.

"Like Scrag said, it was in my hut," Scrag nodded in a confirming manner.

"How did it get there?"

Scrag began to relax a little. Now that Naranda had read the message, she would certainly be pleased that he brought it to her. "A voice in the shadows brought it and said to give it to you and gave Scrag lots of gold . . ."

"Gold? What gold?" Naranda stood up.

Scrag could feel his stomach do flip-flops. He could not believe he had let the part about the gold slip. Seeing a spark in Naranda's eyes, he decided he had better come clean. "Voice in the shadows offered Scrag gold to give you message."

"And you didn't see anyone?" Naranda's voice softened, but it still contained a level of anxiousness.

Scrag shook his head. "No light. Not even goblin night vision could see owner of voice."

The sorceress heaved a large sigh. Scrag hoped it was not because of him. Instead of saying anything, the goblin decided it was best to let his mistress work through it. As it was, the gold did not come up again, and this made him very happy.

He watched as she stood and began pacing the floor, reading and rereading the note. Since Scrag had no way to know what was on the page, he really could not tell if it was just a lot of words or something that was simply hard to comprehend. He doubted the latter simply because Lady Naranda was the smartest human he knew, and he could not imagine anything perplexing her.

She walked around the desk once, then over to one of the overflowing bookshelves. She fingered around the various volumes until she landed on a large book. She pulled it out from the shelf and flopped it down onto the desk with a resounding thud. With keen intensity, she turned the pages examining each one until she landed on one in particular. The expression on her face changed to one of self-satisfaction, and she motioned the goblin over to the desk.

"Are you familiar with Hydesvalley?"

Scrag had to think for a moment. The name seemed familiar, but he was not sure he had ever been there. After going through his scant travels, he concluded he had not ever been in a place by that name. "No, Mistress."

"Look at this map of Fairhaven," Naranda instructed.

"Scrag know Fairhaven. Scrag hates Guardian stronghold. Many failed raids, there." Scrag paused for a moment and tried to anticipate what was coming next. "Scrag need to go to Fairhaven?"

"No," Naranda answered promptly. "Don't worry about the Guardian Corps. I want you to focus instead on the edge of the map to the west of the city."

"What is that small mark?" Scrag asked about the strange markings beneath Naranda's finger.

"That, my goblin captain, is the village of Hydesvalley," she answered. "And this steady line that goes past it and Fairhaven, is the River of Kings."

Scrag swung his head around as if to look out a non-existent window. "You mean river that runs just beyond goblin huts?"

She nodded in the affirmative.

"What's in Hydesvalley?" Scrag knew where he was going, but now he wanted to know why.

"I want you to gather as many assassins as you can gather, put them on a barge, and travel up the river to Hydesvalley. When you get near the docks, just beyond the River's edge, there is a solitary cottage atop the hill overlooking the village. You are to go there and kill everything in sight," Naranda's tone had turned to one of impending victory.

Scrag was confused. Why was she sending him on a two-week journey to an insignificant little village? His eye spotted the magical note now lying on the corner of the desk. What was in the note?

"May Scrag know what the note said?"

Naranda let out a hearty laugh before sporting a devilish grin. He had only seen her smile like this a few times before and only when she was about to succeed at something terribly destructive. "Certainly. The note says that we can find Krestichan's lost treasure in the house of Hammerclaw protected by a Guardian of the Silverwood." She paused and stared at Scrag. "Did that mean anything to you?"

Scrag decided not to play smart and simply shook his head. "All Scrag knows is mistress wants whoever in cottage dead, and that's what Scrag and goblins will do."

"Excellent. Then do not waste time here. Round up your team and leave immediately," Naranda ordered.

Scrag was happy that things ended so well. Not only did he deliver his message and earn a pile of gold, but he was also about to go on a mission in which he would get to do what he was trained to do, kill. As he started out the door of the study, a realization hit him and he turned to speak. "Mistress, a barge will cost money."

"I know," Naranda still worethe devilish grin. "How much do you think will it cost? No, let me guess." Naranda looked down at the paper in her hand. "It's around forty gold coins, isn't it?"

Scrag wondered how she could possibly know, and then everything clicked into place. His shoulders slumped and he turned to leave realizing he had just been duped.

To be continued in Book 1 of the Silverwood Chronicles

Guardian of the Silverwood

ABOUT THE AUTHOR

Matthew Graphman is a twenty-five-year veteran in the information technology world. He studied writing, drama, as well as computers while attending Bob Jones University in the late 80's and early 90's. There he met his wife, Wendy, of twenty-five years and started a family. He currently resides in Bloomington, Indiana with his wife and children, Kathryn (Kat) and Ethan. His oldest son, Sean, is married and lives on the East Coast. Matthew has long been a fan of fantasy fiction. His first attempt at writing was brought on by his roommates in college. As a result, he wrote his first - still unpublished - fantasy novel. After graduating, Matthew continued his writing exploits, but his focus was mostly around theater. After developing a series of children's skits in the 2000's, he was encouraged to take the skits and convert them into a series of children's chapter books. To date, he has written five of the fifteen stories in the "Chel& Riley Adventures" series. Taking a break from creating children's fiction and drama, Matthew decided to reach back, at the request from his daughter Kat, and create a fantasy world that mixed all of her favorite thematic elements. This series is currently outlined to cover five volumes; however, he is convinced that there could be many more stories that evolve out of this new universe. Matthew is a recent winner of the 2016 and 2017 NaNoWriMo challenge, and he is working on the fifth and final installment in the Silverwood Chronicles series.

Printed in the United States
By Bookmasters